CW00864992

SHOW FEVER

Rachel Nobbs

For my mother who asked "What will you write about?"

1
Farm Life

"You know what?" Asked Tayla as she sharpened her HB pencil carefully with a sharper she borrowed from her friend. Ellea waited long enough for it to become annoying and then said "What?"

"Oh, you," said Tayla. She drew a quick and ferocious sketch of Ellea sitting hunched in the haystack "What I mean is our story. It's going to be pretty awesome, I think. What if we win a prize?" she suggested. Ellea pondered while sketching with her pencil.

"Be nice, wouldn't it?"

"What would you spend it on?"

Ellea shrugged. Her tenth birthday was a fortnight ago so she had enough new possessions for a while.

"What would you spend it on?" Asked Mrs Cole coming into the living room with Ellea's baby sister in her arms.

. "Would you two watch Mia for me while I run her bath?"

"Ooh, yes!" Tayla dropped her pencil and pounced on the baby. Ellea sighed it's no use expecting Tayla to say anything sensible now she had Mia to play with.

"Do you think we ought to start copying it out now or wait until Mr Harry's seen it?" She tried.

"Hmmmm?" Tayla was tickling Mia's belly "Ellea how long has she been laughing?"

"Oh, not long. Our story though Tayla! For the competition."

"OH, yes – Mr Harry said we would have some time to work on it this term, didn't he? You might as well start copying it out now though. If we show it to him he'll only say something about 'Are-you-sure-it's-your best-effort-if-so-it's-fine-with-me'."

"Maybe you ought to do the writing out."

"No, you do it. But use your best writing and make sure you leave plenty of room for my illustrations." Ellea grinned. "Fancy that! Us writing a book! With Chapters!"

"Wonder what some of the others will be like?"

"Not like ours," said Ellea "You do the best drawings."
She got up as mother came in with Mia's bath. "Let's
go and feed the horses and foals before it gets too
late" she said "Come on Tayla"
Tayla looked wistfully at Mrs Cole who was
unbuttoning Mia's little pink jump suit.
"Look at her fat little legs!"
Ellea looked but Mia's legs looked the same as usual
to her, As Mrs Cole lifted Mia in to the bath.
"Look she is sitting up!" said Tayla in admiration "she
is strong isn't she, Mrs Cole?"
Ellea waited in the doorway "Coming?"
Tayla followed reluctantly "Wish I had a baby sister"
she mumbled.
"If we hurry," said Ellea, "We'll have time to give Storm
her leading lesson."

The evening was already cool, that's expected for
September. The sun flowers were out in the garden
beside the cow paddock they looked like clumps of
yellow oil paint and Tayla wrinkled her nose at smell
that drifted from the cattle yard. Ellea who was use to
all the smells and sights of the farm, hurried ahead,
boots swishing through the puddles.
"You'd never think that just two weeks ago we were in
the middle of a flood, would you?" she said over her
shoulder. "The river's gone down, now but dad says
he will keep Storm and the others in the paddock near
the dairy for a while yet."
Ellea's hair was escaping from the hair tie by the

time she had finished feeding the calves. She wiped her hands on her jeans and took the horses halter down from behind the shed door "There's just enough time to take storm for a walk!" she exclaimed.

Storm was nearly five months old she shared her birthday with Mia – Mr Cole had given her to Ellea. Storm was friendly foal and Ellea loved her. She slipped the purple halter over Storm's head and tightened it gentle against storms cheek. Then she nodded to Tayla to open the gate. Mr Cole came over from the cattle yard to watch them for a minute.

They headed down to the bottom paddock, first Ellea then Storm with her ears pricked up with enjoyment as her neatly trimmed hooves scraped along the gravel path. Following behind Tayla splashed in any puddle she could find.

"Will she go into a trot?" she asked

"I don't know!" Ellea exclaimed pleased that Tayla was taking an interest in the foal. She jogged a few steps which tightened the halter and she called back encouragingly. Storm was very puzzled. After a few tugs on the rope she got the idea and started trotting alongside Ellea let out a rather loud scream as Storm took off down the paddock dragging Ellea through the muddy wet grass. Tayla watched open mouthed, as Storm was heading full speed towards. Storm stuck her legs out stiffly as she bound to halt at Tayla's feet. Ellea sat down in a muddy puddle of water.

"I didn't mean that fast," Said Tayla

"No neither did I!" Ellea rolled over in the slosh trying to pull herself up.

"I hope dad didn't see us ripping up his grass!" Tayla shook her head doubtfully; her father always saw what they didn't want him to see. Ellea burst in to laughter "I know what it is," she gasped at last "There is storm coming!" Ellea had a chuckle to herself at her own joke, Tayla shook her head and started heading back to the house .

2

Dinner on the Farm

Dinner time on the farm was half past five. "It's only fish fingers, I am sorry" said Mrs Cole, as if Tayla was a grown-up "I was going to make a casserole but it was impossible with Mia" she paused and listened "There she is again" As cry floated in from the bedroom. "Please help yourselves I may be a while!"

"Bet I never cried like that!" said Ellea with confidence.

"No of course not, you were much worse," said Mr Cole "When you were Mia's age-"

"Oh, Dad SHHH!"

"You brought it up" he picked up his dinner knife and began to cut his fish fingers in half.

Mrs Cole finally made her way back into the kitchen "Tayla have you had enough?" Then turned to Ellea and asked "How is your story coming on?"

Both girls glanced at each other before Tayla spoke up "We've sort of got it written,"

"But we have to copy it out "Ellea chirped.

"I hope you will be doing the coping Tayla?" said Mrs Cole

"No I am." Ellea sighed.

"I am doing the drawings," pointed out Tayla

"Would you be allowed to type it up?" asked Mrs Cole

"I don't think so mum!"

"I would love to read it when you're finished!" said Mr Cole

Ellea's father put down his knife and fork. "What is this story about?"

"We all have to write them," said Tayla "In pairs then Mr Harry will send the best two or three into a state wide competition"

"Oh yes, that one!" remembered Mr Cole "Well I am sure it will be great."

Mr Cole turned to the pile of mail beside him and opened the top letter "Ah, the Coast Show schedule," he said

"Are you taking any cattle to the show this year?" asked Mrs Cole

Mr Cole was studying the schedule.

"There is a Dexter feature show," he explained to everyone "So there will be a nice lot of entries this year, it won't just be one big class they seem to have a class for every bred, We might try our luck this year."

"Will you win?" asked Tayla

"Probably not but you have to in it to win it"

"Do you think I could take Storm and enter her in the yearling category in the horse show, Dad?"

Her father ran his finger down the page "Let me see. She was a May foal wasn't she?"

"Of course she was born on the same day as Mia, May fifteenth," said Mrs Cole

"Ahh pity she won't be in the 6months and under then." Said Mr Cole

"She is only four and a half months!" Said Ellea annoyed her father couldn't remember Storms birthday.

"The show is in mid-December," pointed out Mr Cole "This looks more like it!" he began to read "The Owen Clock prize for young foals between 4 and 9 months exhibited by a child under twelve."

"Not too long now" exclaimed Mrs Cole.

"Ages!" insisted Ellea "Heck mum, I'll be nearly ten and a third!"

"Ellea why must you say that?"

"What 'Heck'? Heaps of kids at school say a lot worse, Mum."

Mrs Cole turned to Tayla "Would you like some Ice cream?"

Tayla nodded, but sighed to herself. She had enjoyed writing the story with Ellea and looked forward to inserting the drawings. But knew Ellea may lose interest now she has to prepare for the show.

"Lots of leading lessons and grooming!" planned Ellea

"She could do with quite a few lessons from what I seen today" mumbled Mr Cole

Tayla wrinkled up her nose. She could just see herself trailing along behind Ellea and Storm, just like this afternoon and it's still another three months away!

Mrs Cole paused with the spoon hovering over the ice-cream. Then put it down with a sign. "I can hear Mia," she said.

Tayla jumped up. "I'll go!"

3
Mr Harry

"Silence please everybody!" yelled Mr Harry.
Grade five had been talking and laughing and
making Unsettling noises for the past ten
minutes. The whole class became quiet
everybody liked Mr Harry.

"Mr Harry has had a haircut," whispered Tayla.
Mr harry nodded towards Tayla "I had to," he
said. "My girlfriend was afraid my hair would take
over!"

"Oooohh!" said the year five class.

Ellea smiled at the joke. "This morning,"
announced the teacher, "I'm going to be really
hard on you. I expect you've all been lazy over
the holidays so we will start with spelling
groups."

After little lunch, Mr Harry asked for reports on
the competition stories. Half the class was more
interested in what had just happened at little
lunch.

"Hands up those who have nearly finished," asked Mr Harry.

Four girls raised their hands.

"Half Finished?" A few more hands went up with all the class looking doubtfully at one another.

"And for those who haven't even started yet, they know who they are and they'd better get moving," said Mr Harry. "Get out what you have done and get into your pairs. Anyone who wants to know anything can come and ask."

There was a rustling of papers and a scratching of pencils as the year fives went to work. Ellea took out her rough copy of 'The Storm Story' and the assignment sheet provide by Mr Harry. She carefully began to copy the first chapter. Tayla began to sharpen her coloured pencils.

Mr Harry wandered around and broke the begins of a gossip session and slowly made his way back to the front of the room. He glanced from book to book some were grubby, scribbled on by younger siblings. He looked at Jed and Jacks book which looked like a herd of elephants had trampled over it. He stopped by Ellea and Tayla looking at Tayla's practice drawings. He hesitated.

These books were supposed to be the children's own work but he could see Taylor gluing in magazine clippings and Amy had photos of her chickens in her book.

"If I might just make a suggestion..."he said. Ellea and Tayla looked up. "Perhaps you would like to do some of your own illustrations like Tayla, what about some full page illustrations Tayla?"

"There wouldn't be enough room,"

"What if I gave you some extra sheets of paper?"

"Oh, Thank you!" she said happily "Now I can start working instead of waiting for Ellea.

As the week came to end Mr Harry's desk was piled high with handmade story books, some very uneven others kept neatly in a plastic sleeve. Mr Harry started to think he should have chosen the pairs instead of letting the children choose. By the next Friday Mr Harry had read and assessed all of the books. As there were only thirteen he had no problem picking out the best three.

"The competition closes in a few days," he said, "so I'll post these entries off this afternoon." Taylor's hand shot up as usual ahead of everyone else's.

"Yes Taylor? What is it?"

"Please Mr Harry, which stories are you sending?"

There was a mumble from the class. They all desperately wanted to know. Mr Harry let out a sigh.

"You'll know the results when they come out, if you've won," he said

"When is that?" Yelled Jack from the back of the room. Mr Harry paused. "In the last week of school."

All the children rolled their eyes.

4
Girls will be Girls

All the Competition stories were finished and the
selected were in the mail the rest piled high on
Mr Harry's desk, the term carried on as usual.
While Ellea wasn't at school she spent all of her
time with Storm. She would spend hours on end
brushing the foal with her new grooming kit
which she had saved three weeks of pocket
money for, by far the best twenty five dollars she
had ever spent.

"She certainly looks well," Mr Cole called out
from the diary shed "Don't forget about the other
foals though."

Ellea was in charge of feeding the foals and the
chickens every day, not only did she have to
feed the foals but she had to groom them. Her
father was proud of her and thought she did a
very good job. Ellea was always good at things
she was interested in.

One Sunday afternoon she came in hot and exhausted from helping her father move the dairy cows up to the top paddock. She banged the kitchen door open and couldn't wait for a nice cool glass of lemonade, but she stopped short. In the kitchen there was her mother with Mia in her arms at one end of the table and sitting at the other end was Ma. Ma was smiling at Tayla who was fussing around getting two cups of tea ready.

"Beautiful cups," Ma smiled "That beautiful rose pattern," she said happily.

"We only have those plain supermarket cups at home," said Tayla.

Ma turned in her chair "Oh, Ellea there you are!" Ellea headed over to where Ma was sitting she never liked those kisses were pulls on your cheek, although she knew she would miss them one day.

"And how is Mia dear? "Asked Ma with delight as Mia burst into chuckles of laughter.

"Thankyou dear" Said Mrs Cole and Tayla put down her cup of tea so Mia could not reach. Ellea was very fond of Ma, particularly since Ma had entered in all the shows and had even won at State for her horseman ship skills. Ellea aspired to me like Ma; she looked up to her and knew it was possible.

Although she did not particularly want to sit and listen to her mother and ma talk about babies all afternoon. She looked over at Tayla and jerked her head towards the door "Coming?"

Tayla followed Ellea out of the kitchen when they were out of ear shot; Ellea turned around and said "I didn't know you were coming over today. Why didn't you call? Then you would have been able to help dad and me."

"Mum got called into work, and your mother always says I can come anytime, so mum dropped me off on her way into town."

"Good. We can take Storm for a walk she needs the halter work," Said Ellea "Sorry you had to mix up cups of tea for ma and mother."

"I don't mind," chirped Tayla. "I like that sort of thing"

Ellea turned around a looked at her doubtfully "Really?"

"Yes, do we have to take storm out; can we do

something else instead?"

"Alright" Ellea glanced at her, maybe Tayla was jealous of Storm. But Ellea didn't want an argument so she left it at that. "What would you like to do?"

"Can we listen to some music and dance around?"

"Not with Ma here she would never approve of our music! I know! Let's climb the tree's up near the dairy shed!"

The old gum tree Ellea selected to climb was not far from the house. Tayla looked at the tree with great worry. "How do you reach the first branch?" Ellea climbed up on to the fence post and swung herself up "Come on it's so easy, just like the monkey bars at school."

"we should be wearing sneakers not gumboots" panted Tayla as she slipped and grazed her knee "I'm getting down" she wailed.

"Oh, come on. Look just up here-"Tayla hesitated but followed, they stopped on platform where three thick branches sprouted from the trunk which formed a natural platform. They leaned up against the thickest branch. From their perch they could see everything including the bottom paddocks, house, dairy and even the river.

"Let's build a tree house!" suggested Tayla "This would be marvellous in summer. We could sit up here and do our homework."

Ellea fiddled with the pony tail and thought "Could be fun pity we didn't think of it in the holidays."

"Never mind, there is today."

"And tomorrow."

"And after school."

"What will we need?"

"An axe," said Tayla. "And we will make a rope ladder. We've got some bits of carpet left from doing my room. And a basket to pull things up on a rope…"

They continued to plan happily; Storm did not get any lessons that day after all.

For the next few days Ellea's thoughts were mainly about the tree house they had not come with a name for it. Tayla made sketches of what it ought to look like. It was fun. It was like working on their story again. Spring gradually transitioned into summer the days became much longer and hotter.

Mrs Cole took the girls for a swim in the river; even Mia had a splash in the water.

"I suppose I will have to start helping your father get the cattle ready for the show, How is storm coming along?"

"Oh, well I am taking her for walk today."

"I thought you and Tayla were coming swimming?" asked her mother

"Oh, we'll do that too," announced Ellea.

But they didn't. When Ellea went to storms stable she found the foal lying down in the hay.

"Come on you lazy foal!" said Ellea tugging on the foals halter "Get up!"

Storm slowly got up and took a couple of steps. Ellea stared at her with worry, her stomach started to sink as she saw storm had a horrible limp.

"Seedy toe, I think," said Mr Cole examining the foal.

"Can we get the vet?"

"We shouldn't need to, we have some Tar from when Milly had seedy toe, remember when she was pregnant with storm?"

"Not sure that I do."

"Well I will find the stuff. That ought to fix her up. How long has she been limping?"

"I don't really know," said Ellea "I didn't see her yesterday…" she had just chucked food over the stable door then ran off to see Tayla at their tree house.

"Mm," mumbled her father as he headed off to the dairy shed.

Ellea trailed closely behind, feeling upset. How could she have done this, she neglected her best friend. What if she wasn't better by the show?

5
Coast Show

On the morning of the show, Ellea woke up before the sun was up. Her father is always up milking very early so he is always finished by the time Ellea even thinks about getting out of bed. Together they went to load all the animals for the show. There were two Dexter cows, two calves and a yearling bull, last to be loaded was Storm as she will be the first to get off. Ellea was worried the cattle might slip and fall an squish poor little Storm.

"She will be fine," said her father.

"Now we have just enough time to get breakfast, before we head off."

Breakfast! How could anybody possibly eat?

Mrs Cole was heading into the show later that day with Mia and Ma, but Ellea would be traveling in with her father. She had the biggest smile on her face as she climbed up in to the cab of the cattle truck.

"Slow down chick there is a long day ahead of us," said Mr Cole

Ellea sat on her hands "Are we late?"

"No, just keep your eye on the rear vision mirror and let me know if any of them fall down."

She nodded, trying to control her excitement. It was dimmed however by the fact Tayla had refused to come to the show. She had seen very little of Tayla in the past week except for school. Tayla didn't seem to understand how much work was involved in getting a foal ready for the show.

Things had not been the same since Ellea had found Storm unwell. Usually Tayla and Ellea and such a great time working on projects together like the story and the tree house. The Story!

Ellea had just remembered the results will be
announced this week. Ellea settled down,
keeping a careful eye on the rear vision mirror.

"What are you doing today?" asked Tayla's
mother, making herself a cup of tea. Tayla kicked
the leg of the table as she dropped the crust off
her morning toast on the floor for their family
Labrador coco to eat, as her mother wasn't
watching. "Oh, nothing much mum."
"Would you like to go an visit Ellea? Mrs Cole
says your welcome anytime?"
"No one will be home." Mumbled Tayla "They are
all going to the show."
Her mother let out a sigh wishing she could have
Saturday's off to spend time with Tayla. "Couldn't
you go with them?"
Tayla shook her head "I might do some drawing,"
she said "Could I go over to grandpas this
afternoon?"
"Take Coco for walk she needs he exercise?"
suggested her mother.
Tayla was over taking animals for a walk dogs,

foals whatever she had enough.

The show yard was very empty but side show alley was full of colour and rides spinning around flipping over and loud noise echoing through the alley.

Mr Cole reversed up to the loading ramp. Ellea looked out from the truck cab. She saw a few horses being led around the arena. The tall Ferris wheel looked so high from the cab truck maybe her father would take her later. Last year she wasn't brave enough to hop on but this year was different she was older and much braver, hopefully dad can spare half an hour.

"Come lazy," beckoned her father. Ellea hopped down and helped her father unload storm and walk her to the correct stable, then proceeded to help her father unload the cattle and walk them down to their pit. Once finished Ellea wandered back down to the stable where Storm was being held. She walked Storm out to the wash bay. There were lots of children who all seemed to know each other and were chatting away. Ellea picked up a vacant hose and began to hose down storm. The foal didn't seem to mind the cool water. She pricked her ears with excitement Ellea wasn't sure if due to the bath or her new surroundings.

"Don't take all day with that hose," said someone and Ellea turned around quickly, dribbling water all though her boot. It was a tall rather skinny looking girl, with blonde hair in ponytails. She was leaning back on the wooden fence who looked extremely bored, Ellea blinked and looked again.

"Sorry," she mumbled and handed over the hose. The girl took the hose and didn't even flash a smile; she was then joined by another young boy with the same hair colour. Clearly must be her brother not her boyfriend thought Ellea to herself. Once she was finished she led storm back to the stable which was now labelled PETERS FLAT STORM BIRD.

A shiver went down Ellea's back her hands were still cold from the water, her sock was soaked it made her feel very uncomfortable with every step. Ellea was beginning to wish she had sat down and ate some breakfast. As the day went on she had many jobs to do weather it was preparing Storm or helping her father with the cattle. She was having the best fun she had ever had.

6
Bucking Beauty

A couple of hours later, Ellea was sitting on some hay bales having a rest. Mr Cole was resting on the pitch fork and talking to some of the other exhibitors. Both of his cows had done very well in their class. The rest were not until the afternoon and Storm would be in the last show of the day.

Storm is so clean thought Ellea, she can't be any cleaner than that. Ellea went around and made sure all the animals from Peters Flat had plenty of water, then she started rounded up all of the grooming equipment and putting it back in it's case.

"Why don't you wander off and have a look around?" called out Mr Cole "There is plenty of time."

Ellea shook her head to really enjoy the show you needed someone your own age to walk around with, to gossip to, to giggle with.

Ellea watched from her hay bale as a bunch of teenagers walked past in their bright beautiful dresses.

"Ewe, look at that!"

"Yuck, how can anyone put up with that smell?" They seemed to be enjoying themselves. Ellea hopped down and decided to wander off to buy herself a waffle cone. But it was no fun by herself normally Tayla is there with her it was a tradition of theirs but as Tayla grew older she seemed less and less interested in the show. She stared at the Ferris wheel and decides it would have to wait till next year, or perhaps the year after. She turned around and saw her mother and Ma walking down side show alley.

"Oh, Darling," said her mother, "Would you watch Mia for me? She is asleep and Ma and I would love to have a look around in the pavilion before the judging starts."

"Can't you take her with you?" asked Ellea as she wiped her sticky fingers on her jeans. From the way Ma was looking at her she had better agree. She sighed; after all she wasn't doing anything else. How can she sleep in side show alley though Ellea?

She took the pram handle, Mia was in a deep sleep. With her little chubby hands on either side of her body, her mouth open show off her first tooth.

"Make sure you don't put her in the sun, won't you?" Asked Mrs Cole, she looked closely at Ellea "Are you alright dear? You look very pale."

"Just nerves," snapped Ma briskly "Don't sit in the sun or might be sick after that waffle."

Ellea's tummy churned at the idea, she turned around and started walking off with the pram hoping she would not be sick. Perhaps if she sits in the shade for a while her stomach would calm down. She parked Mia's pram in the shade of the shed maybe she could bring storm out for some company. There was a patch of grass by the fence. Mr Cole watched Mia while Ellea wandered down to the stables to fetch storm. Ellea led Storm up looking for a place to tie her lead rope to. As she searched for a post.

Four horsey people walked past wearing matching polo shirts and hard hats they all had a worried expression on their faces. Ellea couldn't help but think they look out of place in the cattle shed. The horses they were leading looked very expense. One horse was kicking up the grass and seemed a little excited.

Then in a split second, the horse changed its mind and started furiously bucking. Ellea soon realised the horsey people had no control over the mare. She wondered if she should help them.

"Look out!" yelled one of the people

"Get that foal out of the way!" It seemed like they were yelling at her. She wasn't in the wrong and neither was Storm. Suddenly storm pulled back on the rope with such strength, Ellea was dragged back by the pull and the rope burnt her hands. Suddenly Ellea was knocked off her feet and Storm bottled straight towards the bucking mare. There were several screams, She looked Storm was clear of the horse. The horse continued to buck franticly, Ellea looked over to where she left Mia's pram. Mia was in the pram fast asleep but her father as nowhere to be seen. Ellea jumped to her feet "Get out of my way!" she screamed as she raced over to her baby sister.

7
Disaster Strikes

Ellea almost collided with bucking beauty. The air was filled with screams and yells. So many people were frantically rushing about. The horse gave one final buck, which bashed against the pram and knocked Ellea off her feet, then trampled on Ellea's right angle as she came back down. Then shot off towards side show alley.

Ellea was still sitting on the ground, dazed grabbing her ankle, Mr Cole came sprinting over with a look of horror in his eyes a look Ellea knew she would never forget.

"I am going to be sick!" she said weakly. And was.

Mia was let out a big yawn and curled her fingers, how could she have slept through that wondered Mr Cole. A couple of ambulance officers pushed their way through the crowd trying to make their way to Ellea. One of the horsey people was telling Ellea to stand up "Are you right? It doesn't hurt that much does it?" The ambulance men were both kind and gentle to Ellea. They dissolved the crowd that had formed around Ellea. Then proceeded to cut off her gumboot and cut her jeans so they could access the leg. Very gentle they moved her foot in a slow circle. Ellea bit her bottom lip as tears of pain started rolling down her face. Her father hovered over the ambulance officers clutching Mia close to his chest.

"We'll take good care of you," said the youngest officer reassuringly as he applied an ice pack Ellea's ankle. He turned to Mr Cole. "I'm sure she will be alright but I would recommend getting the ankle X-rayed."

While waiting for a stretcher, a reporter came along with her note pad an camera she started talking to Mr Cole and the proceeded to take a couple of photos of Ellea.

And that's how Ellea's picture came to be in the Daily Times Newspaper the next morning with the heading – GIRL SAVES BABY SISTER.

Soon Ellea was starting to feel better after spending a good hour in the ambulance tent, the ice was rapidly taking the pain away from her ankle.

Suddenly she remembered Storm.

"Don't worry, Ellea I will go and look for her," said Mr Cole. He was still holding Mia, as though he was afraid to let her out of his sight.

As soon as Ma and Mrs Cole arrived Mr Cole handed Mia over to Ma, patted Ellea awkwardly on the arm and left.

Storm was found tied to a rail near the cattle pits; she looked up mildly as Mr Cole untied her rope and lead her back to stall. Then hurried back to Ellea.

How much longer until her class is judged?" asked Ellea anxiously?

Mr Cole glanced at his watch "About two and a half hours. But.."

"Good!" interrupted Ellea. "I'll be right by then, won't I mum?"

Mr Cole glanced at Mrs Cole who looked very pale and nervous almost worst the Ellea.

"I don't think so," he began

"You will be going straight home!" said Mrs Cole firmly.

"Can't we wait till after Storms class? Dad will lead her for me, won't you dad?"

"Sorry dear she has to be led by someone under twelve."

"Oh." Ellea said as she let a tear run down her cheek.

"How about young Tayla, is she here?" asked Ma suddenly.

Ellea shook her head. "No she didn't want to come."

"Well it will just have to wait till next year." said Mr Cole briskly, he turned and hurried out. Still nursing Mia Ma ran after him, she huffed and puffed as she grabbed his arm. He listened to everything she had to say and nodded.

"It's worth a try." He agreed "I don't want disappoint Ellea.

"Can I please borrow your phone?"

"It's over there in the truck." Mr Cole pointed to where the old cattle truck was parked up.

8
The Owen Clock Prize

Tayla heard the phone ring as she closed the door behind Coco's wagging tail.

"Oh brother." She muttered, tempted to just let it ring out. But it might be her mother, she sighed and headed back inside, she got to the phone just in time.

Owen leaned up against the arena fence, munching on a Dagwood dog. In the other hand was an ice cold can of Creaming Soda. He was admiring the fact that both of his entrants in the cattle show had won blue ribbons. He picked up his show program flipping through to see when his prize category was on. He thought how disappointed he was that his son was a big CEO and daughter a hairdresser he wished they both were farmers. He started this category because loved seeing that young children were still interested in the outdoors instead of Xbox,

PlayStations or mobile phones.

The prize was a grooming set and a trophy that had been waiting all year for a name to be engraved on it. Owen was judging the category himself, and was looking forward to it.

The microphone crackled as the presenter cleared his throat "Class 21, a foal under twelve months, shown by a child under twelve."

There were twelve entrants in the class, Owen knew most of the children leading the foals, in fact he knew all of the entrants except one. A serious looking girl with smooth brown hair and large brown eyes. She was only wearing a T shirt, jeans and sneakers but still looked neat and tidy.

Owen examined each foal closely as the paraded around the showing arena, pay plenty of attention to the way their owners handled them. To the amount of work had been put in to preparing them for the show. He like little Sammy's foal, but she was a little o the large side. It can't really be under twelve months? Wondered Owen.

He glanced over at the little foal lead by the

stranger. "I know this foal, it's my friend from this morning!" thought Owen. He like the way it had just walked straight up to him so he tied it to a rail near the cattle pits as she was unsure where she belonged. He remembered thinking she must have had a lot of time spent with her. The little girl leading was doing a fantastic job with the foal. Finally after another five minutes, he made his decision. Owen nodded towards the presenter as the contestants formed a line in the middle of the arena.

"This is a very nice class," he began "All the exhibitors have put in a lot of work, even those at the bottom, but I have chosen two that I particularly like," he paused and made up his mind "In fact I have made the decision to award a second prize this year."

"A grooming set to Paula Banks for Mystic Star and first prize goes to Ellea Cole for Storm Bird. Good work to all of you."

The crowd erupted into applause and cheers for both of the girls. Tayla led Storm out of the arena holding on the trophy tightly feeling very proud.

9
Daily Times Headline

Ellea was laying on the couch, staring at the crutches
the hospital had lent her. If an un broken ankle hurt
this much she definitely doesn't want a broken ankle.
The bruise is going to massive in a day or two.
Mr and Mrs Cole had gone into town and taken Mia
with them. Mrs Cole had asked Ma to come over and
sit with Ellea. Ma was making a roast for dinner, a
typical Sunday dinner for the Cole family. Ellea
stroked the Blue ribbon Storm had won, Mr Cole
offered to give the ribbon to Tayla but she refused.
Ellea couldn't believe Tayla lend Storm, she just
couldn't get over it. There was a knock at the door.
"I've got it!" yelled Ma "You stay just there!"
Tayla walked waving the Daily Times in the air with
massive grin on her face. "Have you seen the paper?"
Tayla opened the paper to page two where there was
picture of Ellea being hauled off on a stretcher.
"Oh, no!" exclaimed Ellea
"You will cop it at school."
"I am not going!" said Ellea in a huff
But she had to.

Her mother drove her to school on Monday, feeling very silly as she hopped her way up to the classroom. Ellea quietly snuck in and put her head down on the desk, she could hear her class mates talking about her but pretended not to notice. Mr Harry walked in also holding a paper in his hands.

"I think Ellea and Tayla deserve a big round of applause," said Mr Harry cheerfully "not only did they do excellent at the show but they have won the story writing competition three big cheers!" Ellea raised her head and looked at Tayla they both had a grin from ear to ear.

When the bell rang for little lunch all the children filed out of the classroom, Ellea and Tayla were stopped by Mr Harry "by the way you to that was an excellent story, I knew it would take out first place. If Ellea can manage to stay out of the wars I will arrange for you both to go the presentation next Friday."

Ellea lowered herself down on to the ground in the eating area.

Tayla could not stop smiling, she was so happy she offered to come over and walk Storm every day until Ellea's ankle is better.

"Do you have any plans for the holidays?" asked Ellea

"No, not really."

"How about we write another book in the tree house?"

"Sounds great!"

About the Author

Rachel is a part time writer, who lives in Queensland. With her partner and her various pets. During her recent studies she was inspired to write a childrens novel. She hopes to write many more, with a series on it's way to your book shelf.

Lightning Source UK Ltd.
Milton Keynes UK
UKIC02n2320300718
326528UK00001B/12